minedition

North American edition published 2013 by Michael Neugebauer Publishing Ltd. Hong Kong

Original title: Aesop's Fables
English text adaptation by Martin West
Rights arranged with "minedition" Rights and Licensing AG, Zurich, Switzerland.

Michael Neugebauer Publishing Ltd., Unit 23, 7F, Kowloon Bay Industrial Centre, 15 Wang Hoi Road, Kowloon Bay, Hong Kong. Phone +852 2147 0303, e-mail: info@minedition.com
This book was printed in July 2013 at L.Rex Printing Co Ltd 3/F., Blue Box Factory Building, 25 Hing Wo Street, Tin Wan, Aberdeen, Hong Kong, China
Typesetting in Nofret by Gudrun Zapf-Hesse, for headlines Trajan by Carol Twombly
Colour separation by HiFai, Hong Kong
Library of Congress Cataloging-in-Publication Data available upon request.

ISBN 978-988-8240-52-4

10 9 8 7 6 5 4 3 2 1
First impression

For more information please visit our website: www.minedition.com

Aesop

AESOP'S FABLES

Ayano Imai

THE COCKEREL AND THE JEWEL
THE KID AND THE WOLF
THE OX AND THE FROG
THE FOX AND THE STORK
THE LION AND THE MOUSE
THE HARE AND THE TORTOISE
THE CAT AND THE BIRDS
THE DOG AND THE SHADOW
THE VAIN JACKDAW
THE JACKDAW & THE DOVES
THE FOX AND THE GRAPES
THE TOWN MOUSE AND THE COUNTRY MOUSE
THE STAG AT THE POOL

minedition

THE COCKEREL AND THE JEWEL

A hungry Cockerel, scratching around for something to eat for himself and the hens, found something shining in the ground. Thinking it was food, he dug up the earth eagerly, but was downcast to uncover a jewel. Disappointed, he said to himself, 'If your owner had found you she would have been very happy, but you are no good to me. I'd much rather have found a grain of corn to eat, than all the jewels in the world.'

THE KID AND THE WOLF

A Kid returning from pasture was chased by a Wolf. As he was unable to escape, he turned round and asked: 'I know, Mr Wolf, that you are going to eat me, but I would like to ask you a favor before you do. Please play a tune for me to dance to.' Thinking some music before his dinner would be nice, the Wolf agreed.

But while he was playing and the Kid was dancing, some hounds who had heard the sound ran up and gave chase to the Wolf.

As he ran away, he called back to the Kid: 'This is just what I deserve! I am a hunter, and I should never have stopped to play a tune to please you.'

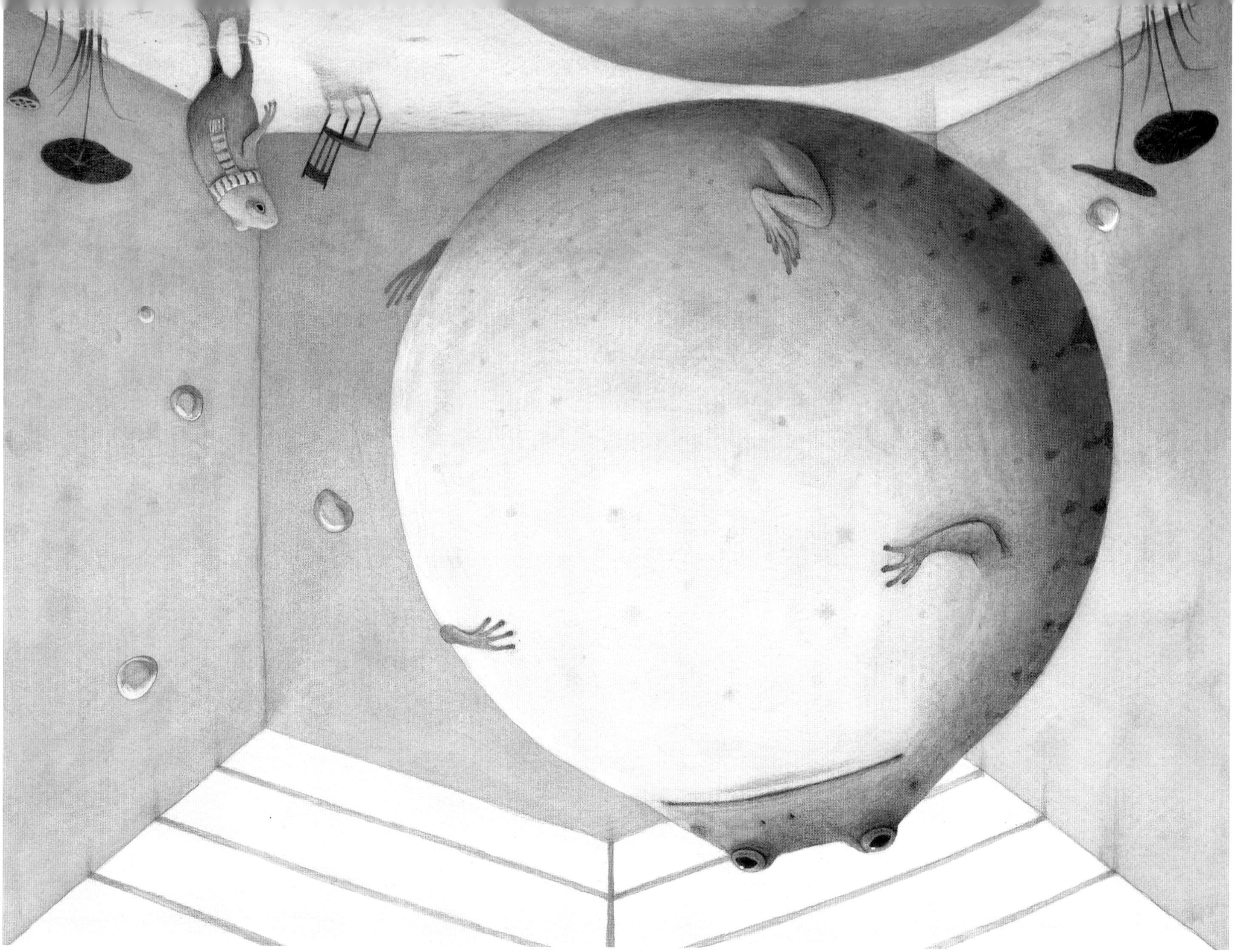

THE OX AND THE FROG

As an Ox was drinking at a pool, he trod on some young frogs, crushing one of them by accident. His mother, who found he was missing, asked one of his brothers where he was. He told her:

'He is dead, mother; just now a huge beast came to the pool and trampled him down with his four great feet.'

'Enormous, was he? Was he as big as this?' said the Frog, puffing herself out to look as big as possible. 'Much bigger,' was the answer.

The Frog puffed herself out still more. 'Was he as big as this?' said she.

'Oh yes, mother, MUCH bigger!' said the little frog.

Yet again she puffed and puffed herself out until she was as round as a ball. 'As big as ...?' she began – but then she burst.

THE FOX AND THE STORK

There was once a time when the Fox and the Stork were very good friends. One day the Fox invited the Stork to dinner and decided to play a joke on her: he served soup in a shallow dish. The Fox could easily lap this up but the Stork could barely wet the end of her long bill in it and finished her meal as hungry as when she began.

The Fox said, 'I am sorry the soup is not to your liking.'

'No need to apologise,' said the Stork. 'I hope you will return the visit. Come and dine with me soon.' So the day came when the Fox came to visit the Stork. When they were seated at the dinner table, all that there was to eat was contained in a long-necked jar with a narrow mouth. The Fox couldn't insert his snout, so all he could do was to lick the outside of the jar and this time it was the Fox who went away hungry.

THE LION AND THE MOUSE

A Lion, lying asleep, was woken up by a little Mouse running over his face. Losing his temper the Lion seized it with his paw and was about to kill it. Terrified, the tiny Mouse begged for his life: 'If you let me go, one day I will repay you for your kindness.' The Lion was amused at the idea that so small a creature could be of help to him and with a laugh let him go. But the Mouse's chance came, after all. Some time later the Lion was caught in a net by hunters. The Mouse heard and recognized his roars of anger and ran to the spot. Gnawing the ropes with his teeth, the Mouse managed to set the Lion free. 'There,' said the Mouse, 'you laughed at me when I promised to repay you; but now you see, even a tiny mouse can help a Lion.'

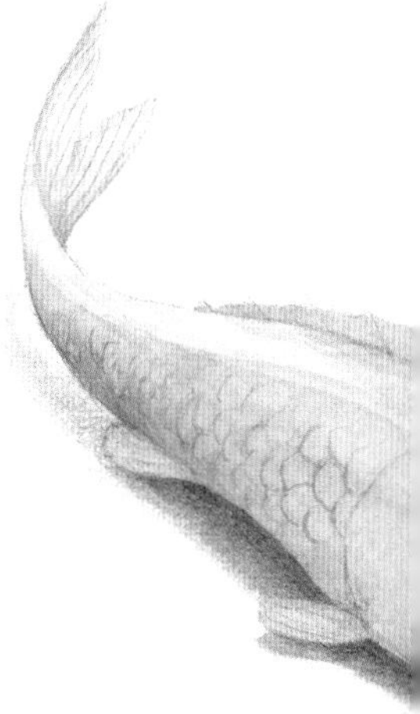

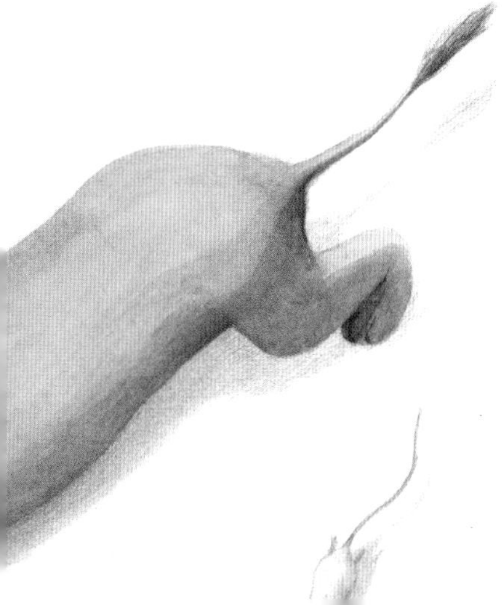

THE HARE AND THE TORTOISE

The Hare was boasting before the other animals how fast he could run. 'I have never yet been beaten in a race,' said he, 'I challenge any of you to race with me.' The Tortoise said quietly, 'I accept your challenge.' At this the Hare roared with laughter. 'That's a good joke,' he said, 'I could run rings round you all the way.' 'Save your boasting till after you've won,' answered the Tortoise. A course was agreed and they went to the start. At once the Hare sped off and was soon out of sight. After a while, the Hare was so far ahead that he thought there was plenty of time, and lay down for a nap. On and on plodded the Tortoise, and in time reached the winning-post. At last the Hare woke up with a start and dashed away at his fastest, only to find the Tortoise there before him. Then the Tortoise said, 'Slow and steady wins the race.'

THE CAT AND THE BIRDS

A Cat, who was really very hungry, heard that some Birds in the neighborhood were ill. So he dressed himself in a fine suit and a white coat to disguise himself as a doctor and, taking a hat and a medical bag, went to call on them.

He knocked on the door and asked the Birds how they were, saying that if they were ill he would be happy to prescribe medicines for them. Without letting the Cat in, they replied: 'Thank you for your concern, but we shall get well if only you will be good enough to go away from here.'

THE DOG AND THE SHADOW

A Dog had seized a piece of meat from a butcher's and was carrying it away to chew in peace. On his way home he had to cross a stream on a bridge. As he ran across he looked down and there in the water he saw his own shadow reflected beneath. Thinking this was another dog, with an even larger piece of meat, he made up his mind to have that as well. So he snapped at the shadow in the water but as he opened his mouth his piece of meat fell out and dropped in the water and he saw it no more.

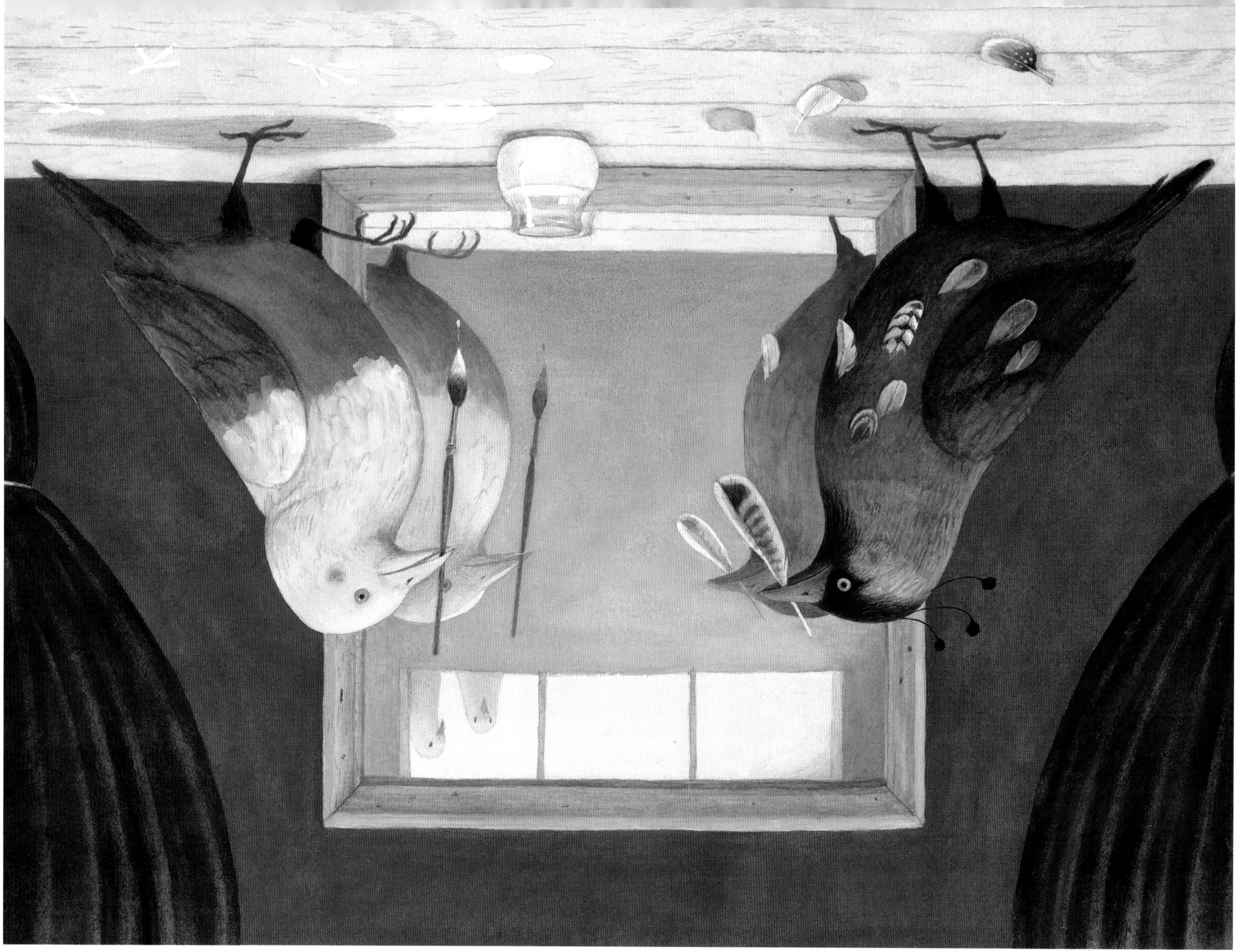

THE VAIN JACKDAW

A beauty contest was to be held, and Zeus announced he would choose the most beautiful of the birds to be king. On the appointed day, the birds flocked to the river to wash and preen their feathers. The Jackdaw, with his ugly feathers, realized he had no chance of being chosen. He therefore waited until all the birds were gone, and then decorated himself with the most fancy feathers they had dropped. When they assembled before Zeus he was about to make the Jackdaw king, when all the birds, recognizing their own feathers, stripped the Jackdaw of his and exposed him for the Jackdaw he was.

THE JACKDAW & THE DOVES

One day a Jackdaw was watching some Doves in a dovecote. 'How well fed they are,' he thought, 'if I could disguise myself as one of them, I'll be able to get a share of their good food.' So he painted himself white all over. As long as he kept quiet they never suspected he wasn't a Dove like them. But once he started chattering they saw through his disguise and pecked him unmercifully so he was glad to join his own kind again. But the other Jackdaws didn't recognise his colour and kept him away from their food. So the Jackdaw ended up with nothing.

THE FOX AND THE GRAPES

One hot day, a Fox found a bunch of ripe grapes hanging overhead which looked all ready to be picked. 'Just the thing to quench my thirst,' he thought. Drawing back, he took a run and jumped as high as he could, but he couldn't reach the grapes. Turning round, with a 'One, two, three,' once more he jumped up, but they were still out of reach. Again and again he tried. Giving up at last, he walked away with his nose in the air, saying, 'I am sure those grapes would have been quite sour.'

THE TOWN MOUSE AND THE COUNTRY MOUSE

Country Mouse invited Town Mouse to visit, to show him country life. He made him welcome, and they sat down to a meal of oats and barleycorns. But Town Mouse said, 'How can you eat this? In my home, I am surrounded by luxuries. Come back with me and see for yourself!' So Country Mouse travelled to town with his friend.

On arrival, Town Mouse showed him the remains of a feast – cakes, jellies and wonderful-smelling cheeses. Country Mouse was delighted and eagerly started to eat. But as they began, someone came into the room. The two mice rushed to hide themselves. When it became quiet, they set out again, but at that moment someone else came in, and they had to run for their lives. 'Goodbye,' said Country Mouse. 'I see you live on such rich food, but there are too many dangers here. I'd rather be at home, enjoying my plain food in peace.'

THE STAG AT THE POOL

A stag, looking at his appearance reflected in a pool of water, greatly admired his beautiful antlers. 'What a magnificent size they are,' he said to himself, 'but I have such miserable thin legs!' While he was admiring himself, a Lion came to the pool and began to chase him. The Stag fled, and was running well ahead of the Lion while they were on the open meadow. But as he came to a wood, he became entangled with his antlers and the Lion quickly caught him. Too late, the Stag reproached himself: 'How foolish I have been! I thought my legs were worthless, which would have saved me, while I gloried in the antlers which have brought about my end.'

[illegible]